A Year in the Country

by Douglas Florian

Greenwillow Books New York

Library of Congress Cataloging-in-Publication Data

Florian, Douglas.
A year in the country / by Douglas Florian.
p.   cm.
Summary: Illustrations with little accompanying
text give a month-by-month depiction of a year
on a farm in the country.
ISBN 0-688-08186-X.   ISBN 0-688-08187-8 (lib. bdg.)
1. Farm life—Pictorial works—Juvenile literature.
2. Seasons—Pictorial works—Juvenile literature.
I. Title.
[DNLM: 1. Farm life—Pictorial works.
2. Seasons—Pictorial works.]
S519.F56 1989   973′.09734—dc19
88-16026   CIP   AC

For my parents

A year in the country...

January

February

March

April

May

June

July

August

September

October

November

December

The year is over—

and a new year
begins.